THE SECOND SON SQUAD

A HEROES COLLECTION SHORT STORY

ALEXANDRIA BLAELOCK

BlueMere Books
MELBOURNE, AUSTRALIA

For permission requests, please contact
enquiries@bluemerebooks.com.

Ordering Information:
Discounts are available on quantity purchases. For details, contact orders@bluemerebooks.com.

The Second Son Squad/Alexandria Blaelock
paperback ISBN: 978-1-925749-85-4
digital ISBN: 978-1-925749-86-1

THE SECOND SON SQUAD

I didn't know where I was, and I didn't know how I got there.

I do know I am, or used to be; a top-notch accountant working for one of the global corporations.

Some might say I am, or was, was one of the most ruthless.

And if some of those knew where I was now, they might say I had it coming to me.

I am now in the body of a teenage girl, who is pretending to be a boy, in an old and elite Military Academy that churns out highly regarded Officers in training.

And it's not like I don't have any urgent issues of my own to manage instead of being wherever the hell I am.

There's money to be cleared through tax havens, gift payments to be made, deals to funnel through shelf companies and trusts.

Exploiting loopholes doesn't just happen by itself.

I think I'm somewhere in Eurasia, but I don't know exactly where. Going by the fashions, I think I'm some time around the turn of the century, say 1910 or maybe 20.

But I don't even know whether I'm on the same planet, or some near-Earth alternative. Geography was never my strong suit.

Somehow, I find being trapped in a near Earth environment more acceptable than having time travelled into another body.

If I believed in reincarnation, I might be inclined to think she is some kind of ancestor. But I only believe in science, so I'm more inclined to believe your consciousness terminates and your body rots.

Or doesn't depending on the embalming.

Regardless, it seemed logical to me, that I needed to resolve whatever unfinished business I found myself in the thick of before I could get back to my own life and resolve the issues that could land me in jail, or dead in a ditch somewhere.

My name was Abby Fisher, but the boys call me Ting Ting, because that, apparently, is the sound a bullet would make ricocheting around my empty head.

Even the Instructors call me Ting Ting, because that's also the sound a thought would make ricocheting around my empty head.

At that stage, I had no idea what my body's actual name was.

Nate sleeps on the top bunk, above my bed. He's the unit's funny guy, a little short, a little overweight, though I thought with the rations and exercise combined, he wouldn't stay that way. If anyone was going to short-sheet your bed, it would've been him.

Zac's in the other top bunk. He already has a body full of scars. He's the one who always runs headfirst into danger without thinking. I thought he'd be the first one killed. Probably in some kind of useless way.

And then there's Locky on the bottom bunk opposite my bed. He's beautiful, tall and blond, with muscles well-concealed within in a layer of thinness. He's so sharp he might cut himself. Sometimes I'd catch him looking at me, and could see his brain moving. I didn't think it would take him long to figure out my secret.

I'm pretty sure they're all boys, our dormitory certainly smells like teenage boys, and I thank god the windows open.

We all make a big show of shaving though I didn't expect any of us have stubble worth the name. I know I don't.

Ting Ting is a little underfed, and not well endowed in the bust department. With her slightly oversize uniform, I think she could get away without binding her chest, though she probably doesn't agree.

And who's to say she's not right, she probably knows the men and boys in this place better than I.

I've been here for a couple of weeks now. I've been following the boys around as I familiarised myself with the layout of the Academy, and worked out where the offices are and where the records are kept.

I say following, but not a lost dog kind of following, more like a kind of lazy, slouchy, dawdling which has resulted in a number of late marks and mild physical punishments.

I've also been sneaking out of the dorm at night, prying into the offices and records which are ridiculously unsecured. Though I suppose aside from spies and 21st-century women, a Military Academy doesn't have anyone to fear.

Firstly, I was trying to find out what Ting Ting's name was, and whether anyone knew she was female.

Secondarily, I was also looking for whatever it was she'd been looking for. Not that I had any idea what that might be.

One night I was sneaking through the school, and I came across Locky standing so still and silent I almost didn't see him.

He was completely unfazed to see anyone else in the corridors out of hours, putting his finger to his lips to indicate I should be silent.

I glided across to where he was standing, and at that point, I could hear conversation from the room behind him too.

"But no one knows where Darcy Dimes is," I recognised the voice of Sargent Walker the commander in charge of the obstacle course.

"It doesn't matter where she is," Sargent Sloane, the strategy lecturer said, "the people will rally around the idea of her."

"Will they?" Walker asked, "Will they really?"

"Of course they will; a princess is a princess is a princess. It doesn't matter whether she's next in line for the throne, or one hundredth," Sargent Thomas, the one in charge of administration and records said, "people will follow her."

I was about to move on; a conversation about princesses had no interest for me at that time, but Locky grabbed my wrist in a vice-like grip and didn't let go.

I looked up at him, his eyes were boring into mine, as cold as the chill in the air.

He wanted me to hear this conversation, and he wanted me to know he'd heard it.

I looked away and wondered was he someone known to me.

Did he think I was Darcy Dimes, whoever this princess was?

I suppose hiding a princess in a Military Academy made a certain kind of sense, but I had no doubt I wasn't Darcy Dimes.

I had a nebulous photo of someone to prove I wasn't a princess. Because carrying a photo of some guy isn't what princesses are known for.

Not that I had found any evidence to suggest who he was. Aside from not being a person currently living in the Academy.

Though there was a small cemetery within the grounds. I'd visited it, but aside from the names and dates of birth and death, I couldn't tell if he was there, because I didn't know his name.

Those that were interred, had all been young, and I wondered if the Academy was more ruthless than I had guessed.

As the days went by, I discovered it was a good place for thinking, to remind myself that Ting Ting, Abby Fisher, and everyone else paid, one way or another, for the lives they led.

And as I subsumed myself into Ting Ting's character, what the consequences might be for me.

I was recalled to my senses by Locky's sharp tug on my arm, just in time to not fall in a heap and get dragged behind him into an alcove a little further down the corridor.

I risked a peek and saw the Instructors filing out of the room. I was curious about Sargent Thomas; I wasn't in any of his classes. I think they were about how to write adequate reports of engagements and incidents. And other conscientious detail-oriented information mentioned in dispatches.

Whereas the other Instructors were lean and seemingly battle-ready, Thomas' physique was more along the lines you'd expect from someone who sat on their arse for a good deal of the day. And I would've wagered he ate perhaps more food than was strictly wise for a non-commissioned officer.

In fact, he reminded me a bit of that weasel Cunningham. I mean it's all very well to have a few gigs on the side, but to expect me to cover up his wrong-doings as well as those of his mafioso boss was a bit much.

Unfortunate then, that he'd caught me in a dalliance with the mafioso's eighteen-year-old son and now had leverage.

Not a sufficiently valid reason to be suspicious, but I reckoned steering clear of Instructor Thomas would be a good thing.

But back to Locky, pressed up against me in the dark, shadowed alcove as the Inspectors filed past.

I knew he was 15, maybe 16 at most. And despite my appearance, I was a thirty-year-old woman.

Who missed her boobs, which was kind of odd as I'd always said I'd get rid of them in an instant.

And without my boobs in the way, he was standing too close. Because I was masquerading as a boy I wondered if he was gay.

And then I wondered if he knew about Ting Ting and thought she couldn't escape him.

And then I realised I had to get away from him before I did anything I might regret.

I slid out from between the wall and his body and scarpered.

But oddly enough, the half-heard conversation about Princess Darcy Dimes stayed with me.

Maybe I felt sorry for her because she was a girl trapped in a life she didn't want. Not unlike me.

Then again, Matilda, the daughter of Henry I hadn't been backwards about coming forwards in pursuit of the English throne.

Hadn't she fled to Normandy on her defeat?

Was the Academy pro or anti-Darcy?

Was she the legitimate heir?

After another exhausting day of lectures and obstacle courses, I went to the library to find out more.

I got out my notebook and skimmed through a bunch of newspapers to find out more about the current political situation. Taking notes where it seemed appropriate.

Externally, there were a number of religious groups, supported by a number of countries.

Internally, the King had been assassinated before I got there, leaving one direct heir, the Princess Darcy who'd gone into hiding.

The remainder of the large and sprawling Royal Family had separated into factions in support of assorted male claimants.

No wonder Princess Darcy had gone into hiding; she appeared to be the key to many a claim, and it wasn't hard to imagine her being forced into marriage to some arsehole bent on running the country, if not the world.

What a shit-storm.

The country had more or less broken into a bunch of city-states.

Princess Darcy was well off out of it.

But.

With my own history of corruption, I wondered about the other major players.

So, I started looking into them.

Oddly enough, my unit comprised sons of the nobility. Josh, Nate, Zac and Locky; all second sons of Dukes or Barons.

I opened a fresh page in my notebook and started tracing the lineages and loyalties.

My unit's fathers formed an interesting web of alliances and enemies such that theoretically, each of the four boys aligned into two pairs of "friends" and "enemies."

And that suggested the unit was formed by design, not coincidence.

Not for the benefit of the boys, but to produce a team their fathers would accept as representing their interests.

All claims to pre-eminence were countered by the others, in terms of rank, they were roughly equal.

I didn't know if it was odd they'd be in a unit together, but it suggested that whoever Ting Ting was, she was impersonating a younger son as well.

The tie-breaker, if you will.

But wouldn't they have known each other? At the very least by reputation, if not having met.

And if they'd known each other, did they also know Ting Ting's actual identity?

Was she really the Princess?

And if she was, did that make me a Princess?

Nothing would suffice, but to open the book at the page describing the King's children.

I kept my eyes closed for the longest time, summoning my courage, before opening them and looking into Darcy's face.

Thank god it wasn't the one I'd looked at while pretending to shave that morning.

That meant I was a decoy.

In the worst case, expendable.

In the best, in training to be a bodyguard or body double for Darcy, with my aristocratic unit.

If we lived that long.

On the bright side, also on the page was the blurred picture I had in my luggage. The deceased Crown Prince who had died in mysterious circumstances a few years ago.

Did I know him?

Was that why I was here?

Locky, or more correctly, the Right Honourable Mr Lachlan Price sat opposite me. "So Lady Abigail, do you remember who you are now? Or why you're here?"

I looked at him.

Hard.

Not one flicker of memory from before I arrived. And any number of hurtful incidents since then.

I lifted my chin, "no, and no."

"That's a great shame," said The Right Honourable Mr Nathaniel Harrison, taking the seat next to Locky. "Keeton's making his move."

"Ah," I said, "Keeton's the one with the money."

"What does that have to do with anything?" asked The Right Honourable Mr Joshua Gatrell, pulling out the seat at the table next to us, spinning it on one leg, and sitting on it backwards.

"Well," my accountant's brain kicked in, "on the one hand he can afford hired mercenaries and assassins, on the other, they're only loyal as long as they keep getting paid."

"How does that help us," asked The Right Honourable Zachariah Turney leaning against the table and crossing his arms.

"All we have to do is interrupt the cash flow and we can bring the faction down."

They looked at me like I was nuts.

And who the hell did I think I was kidding?

How were five teenagers without computers going to achieve anything?

And then Locky said, "I dunno, that might work."

He grabbed an atlas from a nearby shelf and brought it back to the table. He flipped through the pages, then spread it open to the page showing the larger cities across wherever-the-hell it was we were.

"Keeton's chosen the mountain town of Tillia as his base," he said, tapping the location on the map. "He's going to need gold to pay his armies, and the only way it can get there is through the Overhand Pass—"

"And the Overhand is notorious for bandits," Zac said, leaning in to look at the map.

"Call that option B," said Josh, extricating himself from the chair and coming to stand looking down at the map as well. "Who's backing him might be a more important question."

I looked at my notes, "Blaxland, Temby and Semmens."

"That's just the public ones," said Nate, standing up to look at the map, "what about Pusey and Hallam?"

I sat back in my chair and watched them; heads bent over the map talking about how they could put the frighteners on the Lords.

And that's when I realised, they weren't talking about doing it themselves.

Keeton might be buying his army, but these second sons had resources they could draw against - lands, men, armaments. None of it technically theirs, but available for the greater glory of the King.

Or should I say Princess?

And in support of her, the gambit of something for the family, but also perhaps the grant of nobility for themselves.

When the Princess came to power, she would inevitably confiscate lands and maybe put a bunch of people to death. And when it came to the winners, well, she might grant my second sons the titles, lands and people she'd confiscated from others.

And what about me?

While they organised the work and allocated it through their families to take care of, I looked myself up in the book.

Actually, I was using the index, so I looked up five other Abigails before I found Lady Abigail Montrose.

Who went nuts and was committed to an asylum. Her photo showed a woman with a repulsively smug smile, and I wondered if it was taken before or after the asylum.

Before or after she went nuts with grief over Prince Hugo's death.

Before or after she escaped to the Military Academy.

Fairy Tales never tell you about the people trampled by the romance of the main narrative.

And what about me?

Would I go back home and try to extricate myself from the mess I'd got myself into?

Or would I be back in Abigail's asylum looking at the walls?

I frowned as I looked at "my" biography, bottom lip wobbling.

Given the choice, I wasn't sure what I'd pick. Would I get the choice?

What if I was already dead, and this was my karma playing out

Most likely, if I stayed here, I'd be a pawn in some kind of political play. Which actually wasn't that much different to what was happening in my actual life.

I heaved a sigh.

Locky touched my shoulder to get my attention, "are you okay?"

I glanced up at him to see his look of concern.

In fact, they were all looking at me.

With varying levels of sympathy and concern.

A single tear escaped my bleary eyes, and I ran for it. Up the stairs to the second story, back to the classrooms, and into a toilet cubicle.

I really needed a nice glass of red wine. Or failing that, a big block of chocolate.

It shouldn't have been a surprise Ting Ting had got her period.

And given she had no control over her diet, and wasn't taking the pill, that it was uncomfortable. I'm sure some things would have been available had she hidden out in a girl's school, but not in a Military Academy.

And it wasn't like I could stay in the toilet for the next few days, so there was nothing for it, but to get back to the dorm without being noticed, and see what else was in the trunk that might be useful.

I made it to the door of the toilets and found myself on the wrong end of a blunt instrument.

Some time later, I found myself alone in a luxurious bedroom.

By which I mean, lots of space, carpets on the floor, hangings on the walls, a fire crackling merrily in the hearth, a table and chairs, and a lot of bedding.

Sounds cushty, and it was, but the last bed I'd got out of was in amongst four boys, with basically farts and the closed door to keep us warm.

I couldn't help but be deeply suspicious of whoever had brought me here.

And who had taken my clothes, dressing me in some kind of nightie, and leaving me with a dress and a bunch of complicated-looking undergarments?

Rude.

I checked the window, which appeared to be in a tower, and I was no Rapunzel. And the door was locked from the outside. I checked the window again, this time with a view to escaping from it, with next to no further inspiration.

It really wasn't looking good.

There was a knock at the door, and a woman entered with a tray of breakfast things. Outside I saw a soldier, not looking in my direction in case he saw something.

Which suggested that I was someone important, and whoever had brought me here was powerful. And knew who Lady Abigail was.

The woman with the breakfast tray deposited it on the table and gestured at it, then bowed and left the room. I ducked after her, but as expected, two soldiers barred my way. I didn't see any other signs of opponents in the corridor, but it wasn't long, and the soldiers backed me into the room without talking.

If I was a stronger person, I might not have eaten. But I was starved, and there was fresh bread and some kind of jam and some fruit.

Not enough to stick to my ribs and give me strength, but enough to tide me over until I could get something else.

I wolfed the food down, and ignoring the complicated bits, got dressed.

I had no idea what was coming, but I needed to stay calm and keep my wits about me.

In the Academy, we'd been learning to meditate; to focus on our breathing and detach the mind from emotions. To develop a directed concentration and a nonjudgmental awareness of the present.

The aim being to stay calm, focused on the moment, and survive in combat situations.

So, with nothing else to do, I closed my eyes, calmed my mind, and focused on the things I could control.

That being me.

Not long later, the woman came back and bullied me into dressing properly.

Then the soldiers escorted me down the long, winding staircase to the mostly empty great hall.

Where I came face to face with Keeton.

He gripped my shoulders firmly and kissed both my cheeks. Clearly, he and Ting Ting had some kind of relationship.

Which threatened my calm mind for a moment. Especially as he reminded me of that mafioso guy back in my universe.

But soon I was sorting through the implications.

Was I in Tillia?

Had Keeton got word of our plan?

Which one of my boys was the mole?

Keeton escorted me to a table in the centre of the hall with a firm hand on my back. He poured two glasses of wine and gave one to me.

"A toast my dear," he said, raising his glass toward me "to the woman who killed Prince Hugo," and took a sip.

I was in shock, and took too big a gulp of wine and started choking on it. Keeton pounded my back.

"I forgot my dear, you're not much of a drinker, are you? It's one of the things I like about you."

Holy fuck! Not only had I killed the Crown Prince, but I was neck-deep in putting Keeton on the throne.

And there I was thinking I was on the side of right. That someone else was the mole when all along it was me.

Psycho-bitch.

I'd known in my heart that I was too corrupt to be on the side of right. But wouldn't it have been great, just once, to be one of the good guys.

If my second sons knew who I was, were they all traitors as well?

Those poor, sweet, doomed boys.

But wait.

On the assumption I was pro Princess Darcy, we'd plotted out an attack on Keeton. And if they held it together after my kidnapping, it might still be going ahead.

And from what I'd read, Keeton seemed like the kind of guy who stays well back when the fight's on, then strolls in to take the credit.

So, were we "safe" in Tillia?

And could I get away, back to the academy, where I could redeem myself in the eyes of the others?

First things first, I had to get away from Keeton.

Which was actually fairly easy.

One last pound on the back and I vomited up the wine on him. When he tried to jump back out of the way, he knocked my arm, and I spilt the rest of it on both of us.

And landed on my knees in the worst of the mess, and then fell to my hands and knees and apologised profusely for the mess.

I thought for a moment he was going to kick me, and I have no doubt that he would have if I wasn't still useful to him.

But it suited his vanity to have a woman on her knees before him, so he sent me away to change and rest for dinner.

And while it would have served her right to marry him, I really hoped, just in case I was still here, that he wouldn't have her.

He left in a swirl of sandalwood scented finery, neglected to instruct anyone to take care of me, and therefore I became no one else's business.

I made my way to the basement on the assumption the laundry would be near there, and I was lucky enough to find some unattended clothing.

Not lucky enough to find clean clothing, but now that I knew I was a killer, I knew I deserved nothing more than someone else's filthy clothing.

I folded up something like a loin-cloth and changed my clothes.

And looking like some filthy boy, it was ridiculously easy to leave the castle.

Surely someone should have been watching?

Then again, I can't say the Academy actually encouraged independent thinking of any kind.

I'd been hoping to sneak away, follow the path down the mountain, and eventually find a train that would take me back to school, but I realised I had no idea where it was.

Nor did I know the name of the Academy.

Which put a bit of a crimp in my escape plan.

Should I hang around in my disguise in the hope of finding something to sabotage?

Or would my impromptu action harm the second sons' plan?

I was so angry at myself for being a traitor, I just wanted to burn the building down.

I wondered if I could find the armoury, or more particularly, the powder magazine. I started looking around for it.

The powder would need to be kept dry, and well away from anything that might create a spark. It would need thick walls, and possibly a reinforced roof. Or maybe it would be partially buried.

If you were sensible, it would be in an isolated position a little way away from the castle.

If you were less than sensible, you might leave it loose in the basement.

Either way, it didn't seem likely I'd be able to set fire to it without losing my life.

Then again, what about cartoon physics? Couldn't I set a fuse by knocking a hole in a keg and drawing a long line of powder? Theoretically yes.

And how would I light it?

Pipe smoking was common, could I steal a lit pipe, tap the embers out on the trail of gunpowder and make a run for it?

As good a plan as any. All I needed to do now was to figure out how to carry 75 litres of gunpowder.

I ruled out strapping it to an animal immediately.

And that meant I needed someone to help.

In the stronghold of my enemy, I needed someone to help me blow it sky-high.

Jesus wept, as the mafioso's girlfriend might say.

All right, I told myself, calm down.

Take a deep breath, calm yourself, and detach yourself from emotion. Just watch the people milling around you, and let your intuition guide you.

I spotted a little hut not far away that was probably it.

I looked for guards and became aware of a boy on the other side of the yard, who appeared to be looking at me. He was filthy but in the kind of way that looked like he'd dabbed on a bit of dirt as if it was makeup.

He looked kind of familiar.

He looked like Locky.

I flashed our secret signal gesture, and he flashed it back.

Thank god.

I shrugged my shoulder in the direction of the powder magazine, and he started walking over there.

I checked no one was following him, then started walking in that direction too.

We looked at each other for what seemed like forever.

"What's the plan?" he asked.

I sketched it out for him, and he looked doubtfully at me but shrugged his shoulders.

"Let's give it a go."

"Are the others with you?"

"No. We've got a mole and I didn't want to take any chances."

"Ah.

"I found out who it is," I said, "and it's me."

He said nothing for a moment.

"You've changed recently, and I can't put my finger on what it is, so I'm going to trust you. But if you've betrayed us, I will kill you myself."

I was tempted to make a joke about his battle training, but I said, "better you than anyone else."

It made me feel slightly better for it to be him; he was an excellent shot and I wouldn't suffer.

I couldn't believe we managed to get it all set up without anyone noticing anything out of the ordinary.

My shoulders were itching the entire time, waiting for someone to fire a shot into my back.

There were so many things that could have gone wrong with the plan I was loathe to leave it. But I couldn't let Locky sacrifice himself for my stupidity.

He lit the fuse, and I grabbed his hand and started running.

Down the bailey, through the curtain wall, across the drawbridge, and on our way down the mountain.

I thought my lungs would explode by the time I felt the ground rumble and felt the shock wave knock me off my feet.

«« • »»

I didn't know where I was, or how I got there.

I was in a white room, and Nuns I guess they were, were tending my wounds.

Which were extensive.

I'm told Queen Darcy visited me in my room and had helped tend my wounds before she passed her judgement.

For the murder of her brother, my penalty was death.

For the decimation of her main rival, and promotion to Queen, my penalty was commuted to life.

Not at the asylum, and not at the Nunnery.

Cast out to live alone on some island in the middle of a lake.

No doubt when I was more myself, whichever self that was, there would be some kind of paper documenting the punishment.

I wasn't upset about it, in fact, I was looking forward to it. A really nice long spell of time on my own. To think, and maybe write.

But that wasn't it at all.

According to the Who's Who, Lady Abigail Montrose the Prince Killer was dead. No doubt about it, blown up at Keeton's Castle thanks to the bold plan of the second sons.

But, the Queen had given me a new identity.

The Honourable Lady Ava Price, Lachlan's long-lost cousin.

And the new Ting Ting had a place at the Academy for the next term too.

I'm not sure why I'm still here.

But I'm going to enjoy it while it lasts.

THE END

ABOUT THE AUTHOR

Alexandria Blaelock writes stories, some of them for *Ellery Queen's Mystery Magazine* and *Pulphouse Fiction Magazine*. She's also written four self-help books applying business techniques to personal matters like getting dressed, cleaning house, and feeding your friends.

As a recovering Project Manager, she's probably too fond of sticking to plan. She lives in a forest because she enjoys birdsong, the scent of gum leaves and the sun on her face. When not telecommuting to parallel universes from her Melbourne based imagination, she watches K-dramas, talks to animals, and drinks Campari. At the same time.

Discover more at www.alexandriablaelock.com.

BOOKS BY
ALEXANDRIA BLAELOCK

SHORT STORY COLLECTIONS

The Histories of Hayward Hall
Lovelorn, Lovestruck and Love at First Sight
Common or Garden Variety Heroes
Case Files of the Wilkinson Detective Agency
Unavoidable Fates

OTHER FICTION

That Love Nonsense

MS BLAELOCK'S BOOKS

Stress Free Dinner Parties
Signature Wardrobe Planning
Holistic Personal Finance
Minimally Viable Housekeeping
Planning a Life Worth Living

SELECTED SHORT STORIES

Alma's Grace
Balancing the Book
Carmelita Basingstoke
Fate in Your Hands
Kiss of Death
Lady of the Looking Glass
Life in the Security Directorate
Long Weekend in the Snow
Love in the Past Tense
Love in the Security Directorate
Morning Star, Evening Star, Superstar
Needy Bitch
Payton's Run
Phoenix Child
Secret Singer
Shining Star
Ship in a Bottle
Simone Says Hands in the Air
Special Relativity in Space
The Bygone Boyfriend
The Day the Schedule Broke
The Ghost Detectors
The Guardian's Vigil
The Mince Pie Mystery
The Mystery of the Master Suite
The Pseudonym's Bride
The Shadow Thieves
The Time-Space Paradox
Toy Soldiers